D0786229

THIS IS MY EYE

A NEW YORK STORY

Pictures and text by

Neela Vaswani

Candlewick Press

My dad says it's not what you look at—

it's what you see.

This is what I see.

DC VARIO-ELMAR 1:3.3-6.4/4.3-129 ASPH.

When I spin, everything blurs.

On windy days, the city leans

and flies.

Puddles are mirrors.

Walls tell stories . . .

Grown-ups
are
Obsolete

and stories are everywhere.

CERNESTO.
2013
YMi TWD

From my back, I watch the sky.

To see the ground, I just flip over!

Things look different through a fence.

Through the peephole, Grandma is tiny.

Rainy days have polka dots.

A picture is a moment . . .

a moment . . .

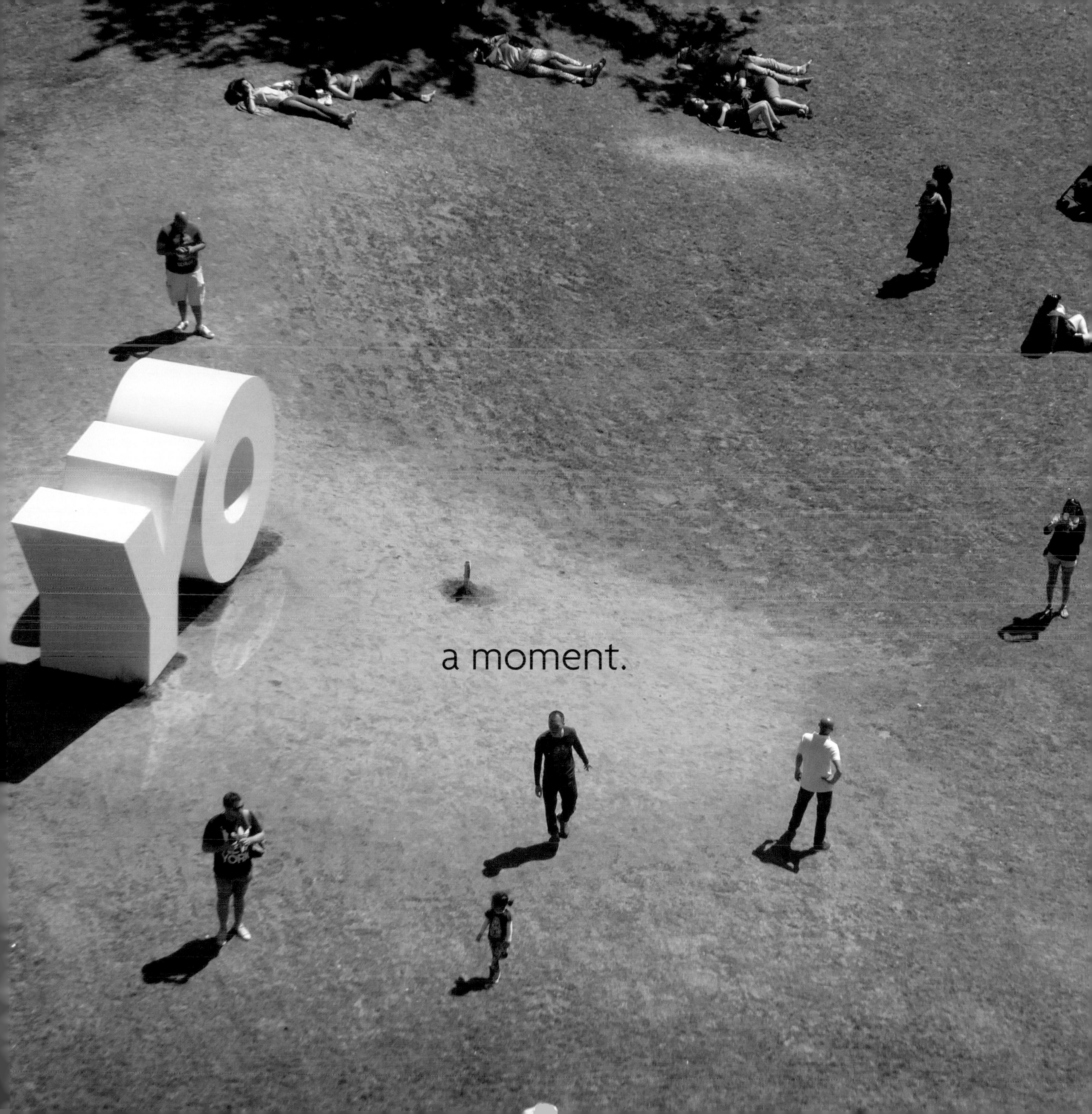

a moment.

There's a dragon in my neighborhood.

This is a mystery.

Trees are comfy.

Statues, too.

Shapes and patterns are everywhere.

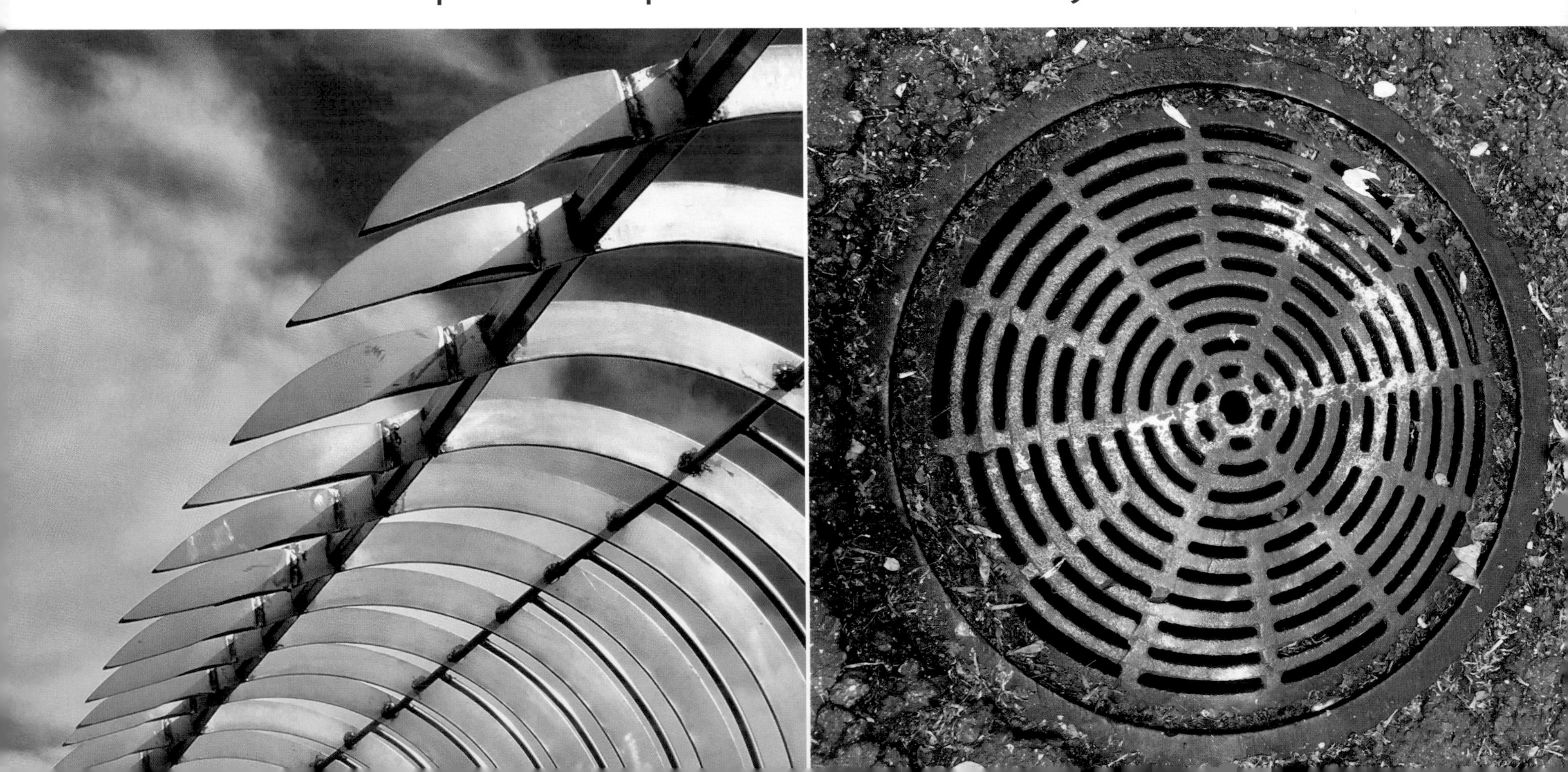

Someone fit
these together.

A shadow visits.

This is someone's art.

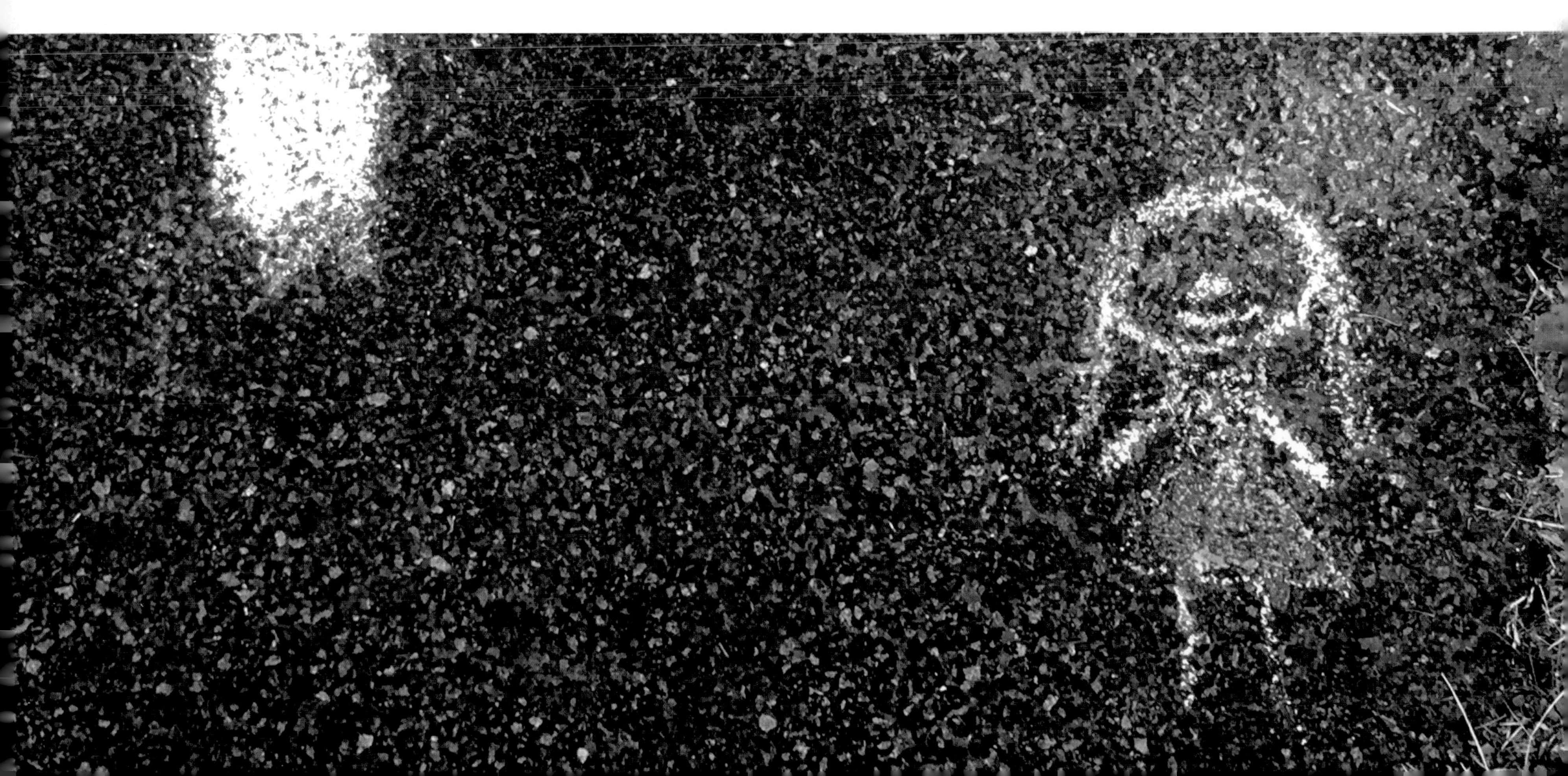

Red shouts!

Orange is quieter.

Blue chairs are for daydreaming.

Underwater is another place.

I like hands

and paws.

On the ferry, I am a seagull.

Goodbye,
subway station.

NEW YORK UNIV

Up is down,

and down is up.

This is what happens when I have a big sneeze.

From up high,
the city stretches.

Little things grow in little spaces.

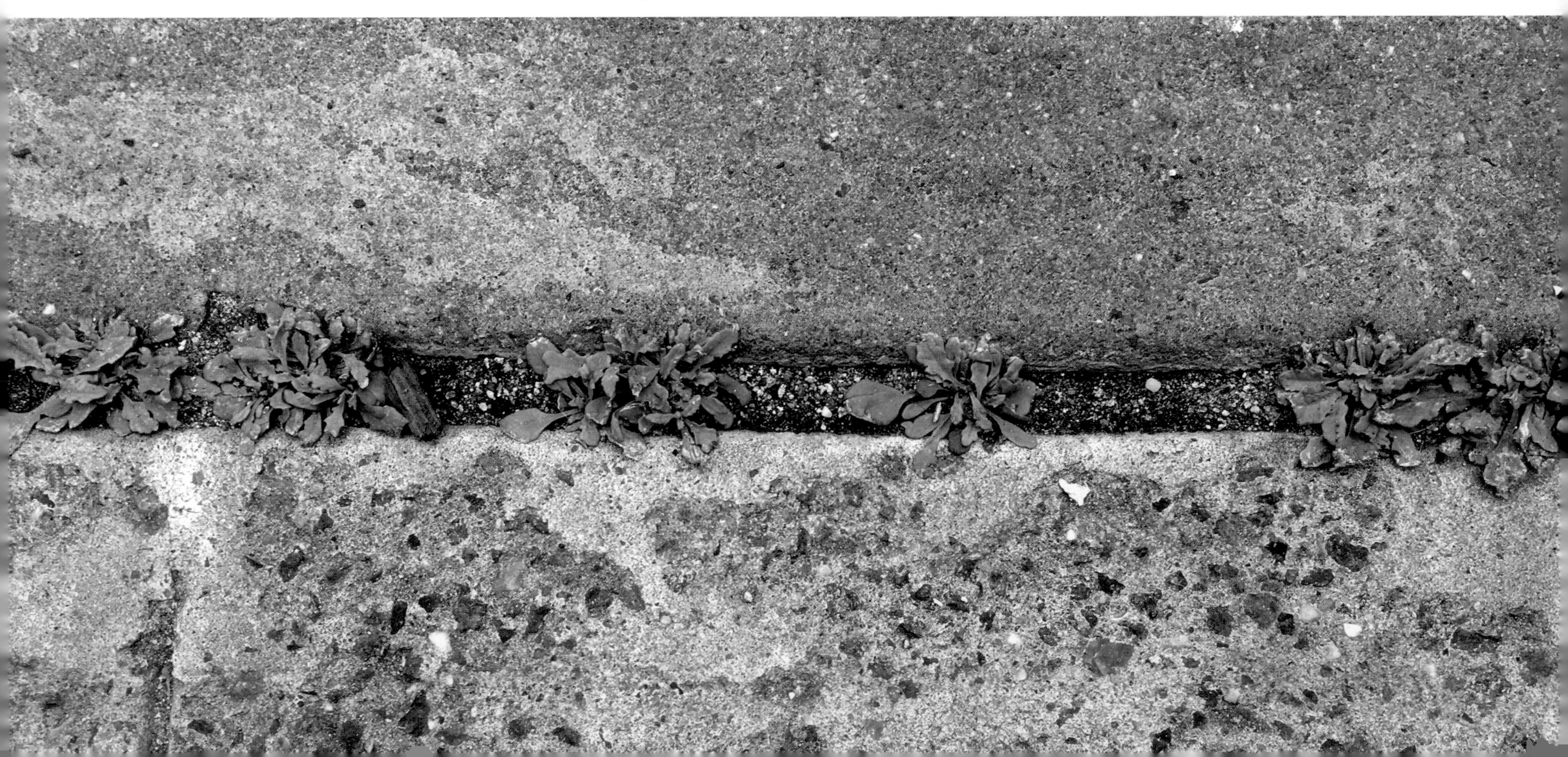

My garden.

Our moon.

My right eye closed.

My left eye closed.

Open both to see my everything.

AUTHOR'S NOTE

Point. Click. Shoot. Which New York is this?

As a writer, I love to slip into the minds and souls of the characters I create. It was wonderful to also be the photographer for this book: I had to see the world as my nine-year-old character would. Kneeling or squatting to take a photo (so I was closer to the ground like a child) changed my perspective. I spun, I swam, I played with my camera. I had to be free, less careful, and more creative with angles, color, and light.

I took photos to match the text I'd written, though sometimes a picture would ask to be taken and new words would come from those photographs. I wrangled friends and family as models (a few of whom took pictures in the book) and wandered all over the city, from Vinegar Hill in Brooklyn to Southern Boulevard in the Bronx. It was important for me to capture the city as a character. I also wanted the photographs to reflect the vivid, in-between eye of a girl who comes from a family like mine, the kind of family I didn't see in books when I was a child.

The world looks different depending on who you are and where you come from. It's my hope this book will inspire kids to think about their own points of view. How would you tell the story of your life and town in photographs? What would you choose to capture? Find out: take pictures!

FOR JIM

More than half of the photos in this book were taken on a smartphone; the rest were taken on a refurbished digital SLR camera.

 First edition 2018. Library of Congress Catalog Card Number pending. ISBN 978-0-7636-7616-2. This book was typeset in Agenda.
Candlewick Press, 99 Dover Street, Somerville, Massachusetts 02144. visit us at www.candlewick.com.
Printed in Shenzhen, Guangdong, China. 18 19 20 21 22 23 CCP 10 9 8 7 6 5 4 3 2 1